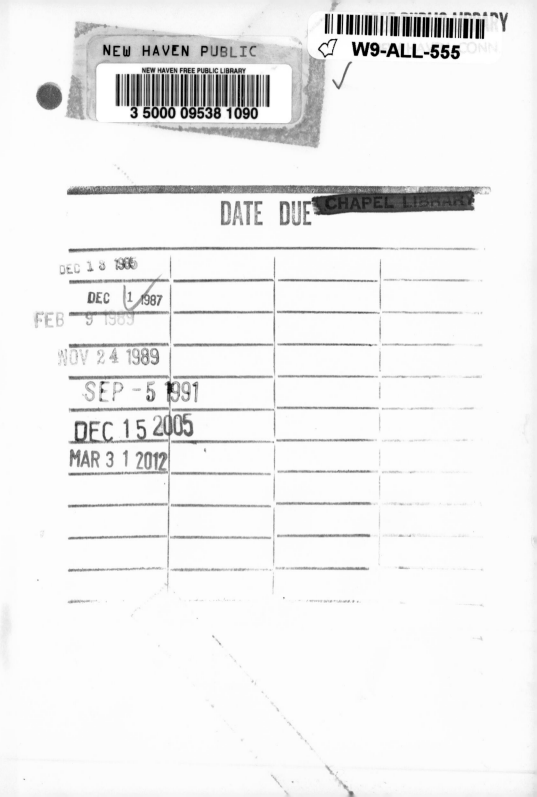

WARTON AND
THE KING
OF THE SKIES

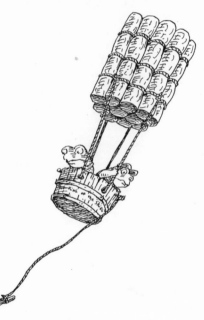

WARTON AND THE KING OF THE SKIES

by RUSSELL E. ERICKSON

pictures by
LAWRENCE DI FIORI

Lothrop, Lee & Shepard Co./New York

A Division of William Morrow & Company, Inc.

Library of Congress Cataloging in Publication Data
Erickson, Russell E
    Warton and The King of the Skies.
    SUMMARY: Two toad brothers gain their freedom from a bickering weasel family by teaching them the value of teamwork.
    [1. Toads—Fiction. 2. Weasels—Fiction. 3. Brothers and sisters—Fiction] I. Di Fiori, Lawrence. II. Title.
PZ7.E7257Was   [E]   78-4919
ISBN 0-688-41852-X   ISBN 0-688-51852-4 lib. bdg.

Also by Russell E. Erickson

Warton's Christmas Eve Adventure
Warton and Morton
A Toad for Tuesday
The Snow of Ohreeganu

Except for the chirp of a small bird now and then, there was but one other sound that broke the stillness of the deep forest. It came from the bottom of a giant twin hemlock where Warton the toad, wearing faded brown shorts and a green sun visor, was busily beating the dust out of a braided rug.

The rug was draped over a line strung from the hemlock to a stump that hid the entrance to the home Warton shared with his brother, Morton. Although Warton always enjoyed doing his cleaning chores—just as Morton always enjoyed doing his cooking chores—he was very glad to be nearly done, for it was the hottest day of the summer.

Never had the sun burned brighter. It was only mid-morning, yet open fields were already sending shimmering waves of heat towards the blue sky. In the forest the leaves of the big oaks and maples hung limp and the tips of the evergreens drooped.

On the forest floor the dark earth was warm, and the air hung still.

Warton gave the rug one last whack, then, satisfied that he had not missed a single speck of dust, he rolled it up, threw it on his back, and entered a hole in the stump. He followed a tunnel downward till it stopped at a small door. Pushing it open, he stepped in just beside the kitchen sink.

Morton, with a damp towel wrapped around his head, was filling a pitcher with cold water that trickled down from the wet, mossy rocks above their home. "I've made some fresh huckleberryade," he said. "If you have time, I'll pour you some."

"I've plenty of time," said Warton, as he put the rug in the parlor. "I've just finished my cleaning for today."

"And none too soon, I'd say," said Morton. "I've never known it to be as uncomfortable as this, even underground."

"When it's this hot," said Warton, "there's only one thing to do." He went to the cellarway and came back with a large wooden washtub, which he half filled with cold water. Then, taking a tall glass of the huckleberryade, he sat down in the tub. "Ahhh," he sighed, "this is perfect. Why don't you get the other tub, Morton? It's very refreshing."

"Not me," said Morton. "I'll drink my huckleberryade here in the rocker."

Warton, feeling quite content, leaned back and shut his eyes. When he opened them he saw that Morton had a wistful smile on his face.

"I'll bet you're thinking of the wintertime, and the snow and ice," said Warton.

9

"No," said Morton. "I've been thinking about something I've often thought about before. It must be the most wonderful and relaxing way there is to cool off."

Warton's eyes widened with interest.

"Do you remember the time we climbed the boulder behind cousin Alfred's," continued Morton, "and how we could see the red cliffs far off on the other side of the forest?"

Warton nodded.

"Then you must remember how we could see the hawks that lived there," said Morton. "How they seemed to float so easily, high over the tree-tops, and how they circled round and round, drifting on the gentle winds without moving their wings in the slightest."

Warton looked at his brother. "You think of that often?"

"I know it's silly, but I've never forgotten it," said Morton. "It must be so peaceful, so pleasant, drifting high over everything." Then, with a sigh, he got out of his rocking chair and went to the pantry.

"Hmmm," said Warton as he took a sip of huckleberryade. "Hmmm," he said again, after he got out of the tub and dried off. For the rest of the morning he was much quieter than usual. Every once in a while he murmured, "Hmmm."

At lunchtime Warton was deep in thought.

"Is something wrong with your B.L.M.?" asked Morton.

"Oh, no," said Warton, "it's the best beetle, lettuce, and mushroom sandwich you've ever made." Then he grew silent again. As soon as he finished eating, he told Morton he was going outside.

"In this heat?" said Morton with surprise. But Warton had already disappeared into the tunnel.

As soon as Warton stepped outside he began poking about in the underbrush. When he came upon several large puffballs he picked one up, emptied out all its powder, and threw it into the air. It quickly settled to the ground and bounced under some ferns.

"Too heavy," muttered Warton.

Next, he hurried down the open hillside to the

pond. At the water's edge he spied an empty goose egg. "This could be just what I need," he said, tossing it as high as he could. It landed with a plop at his feet, and Warton shook his head.

He started searching again, and was in amongst some cattails when he discovered a deserted duck's nest. From the old feathers lying all about he carefully chose a few of the downiest, and tied them together with a piece of vine. He held his breath and tossed them up. They returned quickly to the ground, and he looked very disappointed.

Dejectedly, Warton started back up the sizzling hillside. By the time he reached the top, he felt so wilted he decided to cool off in the little stream that ran nearby. He gave a leap and landed far out in the middle. For a long time he swam round and round, slowly kicking his legs in the clear green water. Then he climbed onto one of the rocks in the stream. Once again he fell into deep thought.

He was staring absentmindedly at the stones along the water's edge when his eyes opened wide.

"There's the answer!" he cried, hopping to one of the stones. Carefully he picked up his discovery and headed for home.

"Now," he said to himself as he hurried along, "I think the best place to build this will be on top of the hill that overlooks the clover meadow. There's always a breeze there. And I'll begin tonight, right after supper."

Morton was just setting the table when Warton returned. As soon as Warton washed up, the two brothers sat down. Morton had made a hot-summer-night supper, cool and light, but very nourishing. It was one of Warton's favorites. First there was a bowl of chilled snail soup. Then came a huge tossed salad of cucumber beetles, cabbage worms, and corn borers. And for dessert, they each had a frosty scoop of iced dewberries.

"Delicious," said Warton, giving his stomach a pat. He went into the cellarway and brought out the big wooden washtub. "And now I'm going outside. I have work to do."

"And you need the washtub?" asked Morton.

"Right," said Warton. "Also some rope, some heavy yarn, a strong needle, my tool belt, and my carpenter's hat."

Morton watched silently as Warton put the things into the tub and started up the tunnel. He had learned long ago that once Warton got an idea in his head, there was no stopping him. "I think I'll go next door for a game of checkers with Grampa Arbuckle," he muttered.

Once outside, Warton grabbed one of the handles of the tub and dragged it along the narrow path till he came to the top of the hill that over-

looked the clover meadow. Except for the grass and an old hollow stump, the hilltop was completely bare.

"I'll build it near that stump," thought Warton. "And when I'm done I can store it inside." He put on his tool belt and carpenter's hat, unfolded his ruler, and set to work.

As he worked, he enjoyed the sweet smell the warm breezes carried up from the clover meadow, and he whistled a little song. After a time he noticed that the sun had turned the color of ripe raspberries and would soon settle behind the hazy hills.

"I hope I can finish tonight," he said. He worked till the first star twinkled in the darkened sky and the sound of crickets filled the air. At last he gave a grunt of satisfaction. "There!" he said. "It's done!"

Carefully, he put what he had made, along with his tools, inside the hollow stump. "When Morton sees it," he said to himself as he started along the path towards home, "he's going to have the surprise of his life!"

The next morning, to Warton's delight, was even hotter than the day before. After breakfast, as Morton was doing the dishes, Warton said, "If ever there were a day when one needed to cool off, it looks as if this is going to be it."

Morton just nodded as he put away the last dish.

"It would be pretty nice to float along up in the sky today, eh, Morton?" said Warton, trying not to smile.

"I suppose so," said Morton, not paying much attention.

"Say," said Warton, "how about taking a little walk with me this morning? There's something important I'd like to show you."

Morton looked at his brother's eager face. "Oh, all right," he said. "But I'm not going far in this heat."

"The heat won't bother you for long," chuckled Warton under his breath.

Morton followed Warton up the tunnel and along the narrow path, every once in a while muttering, "What's he gotten into his head now?"

When they came to the top of the hillside Warton led the way straight to the old stump. "Now, shut your eyes," he said.

After he was sure Morton was not looking, he reached into the stump and took his tool belt and hat and put them on—just in case he had to make any last-minute adjustments. Then he pulled out what he had made the night before.

"Okay, Morton," he said, "open up!"

Morton opened his eyes. "What...what is it?" he cried.

"It's what's going to take you up into the air," replied Warton, "where you can float around and be cool and calm."

Morton gasped and looked again at the strange contraption. He recognized the wooden washtub right away, but he wasn't at all sure what it was that was attached to it, and which Warton, it seemed, was having a hard time keeping from drifting away. "What is it?" he cried again.

"Well," said Warton proudly, "those tubes, which are the most important part, are made from a dried snakeskin I found. It's the perfect material—light but strong. I cut it into several pieces

17

and sewed one end of each piece shut. Then I fastened them all together like a bunch of cigars and attached the whole business to the tub. As you can see," he said, struggling to keep his feet on the ground, "the slightest breeze blows right into it, and it's just itching to shoot up into the sky. All you have to do is hop in."

Morton looked terrified. "But...but," he stammered.

"Don't worry," said Warton as he hung a whistle around Morton's neck, "I have a strong rope attached to the tub. When you want to come back, just whistle and I'll pull you down."

Morton swallowed hard as he stared at the strange balloon. He looked up at the sky, then back at the balloon. As his eyes darted back and forth they seemed to grow wider each time. At last, he shook his head. "I'm ... I'm very sorry, Warton," he said, "but I'm afraid I simply cannot ..." Morton suddenly stopped speaking. He was noticing for the first time what Warton had neatly painted on the side of the tub: *The King of the Skies.* Morton choked a bit and he looked at his brother, who was absolutely beaming. Then he took a deep breath and said, "I'm sorry, that is, that you didn't think of this sooner, Warton."

"Me too," said Warton. "But I never knew you wanted to fly."

Morton hopped over beside the tub and put one foot inside. He looked at Warton, then nervously put his other foot inside. Immediately, Warton looped the rope over a stub on the stump. Although the breeze that swept the hillside was very gentle, it nevertheless filled the snakeskin tubes, making them swell till they were like stuffed sausages. Quickly they righted themselves in an up-and-down position over the tub. The rope grew tight and Warton began to release it. The tub quivered and slowly lifted off the grass.

Morton shut his eyes and held on tightly to the sides. The snakeskin tubes above him flapped and crinkled as they moved through the air. The tub swayed gently back and forth. A soft breeze that was brushing over Morton began to feel cooler. And then there was a sudden jolt. "Oh, no!" cried Morton. "I'm falling."

His eyes popped open, and he saw the blue sky above him and all around him. He saw puffy white clouds that were closer to him than they had ever

been. He saw a lone crow drifting by, but it was
not above him, it was *beside* him.

Morton peered cautiously over the side of the
tub, and gasped. For he was looking down upon
the spires of the forest pines, the swaying grass of
the fields, and the sparkling water of the pond.

"It's beautiful!" he exclaimed. Suddenly, he
pinched himself. "And it's not a dream!" he cried.

As he looked all about, a wide smile spread
across his face, and he sat that way for some time in
the peaceful, cool, quiet sky.

"This is wonderful," he said aloud. "And to think I didn't want to get into this contraption that Warton made just for me on the hottest day of the summer." Then Morton blew loudly on the whistle.

Warton began pulling on the rope, and soon Morton was back on the ground.

"What's wrong?" asked Warton. "Didn't you like it?"

"Like it?" said Morton. "It's the most wonderful thing in the world. And I want you to take a ride in it."

"Oh, no," said Warton. "I made it for you."

"Please!" pleaded Morton. "I'll feel selfish if you don't."

"All right," said Warton, who could hardly wait to try it.

Morton got out and handed the whistle to Warton as he jumped in.

"Now just let the rope slip over that stub on the stump," said Warton. "And don't worry. It's tied tightly at the end."

Warton had no more than gotten the words out

of his mouth when an extra strong breeze whipped up the hillside. It caught the snakeskin tubes square on and, with a jerk, the little craft lifted into the air.

Morton watched the rope fly over the stub of stump. When it came to its end he saw the sturdy knot that Warton had put there. But then, to his horror, as the rope pulled tight, there came the sound of breaking wood. The stub broke off the stump, and the end of the rope went whizzing across the grass.

Without a moment's hesitation, Morton gave a tremendous leap and grabbed the end of the rope. He pulled against it as hard as he could and dug his feet into the hillside. But the wind was too powerful, and Morton found himself being lifted into the air.

Warton was settling back to enjoy the magnificent view when he heard terrified cries coming from beneath him. He leaned over the edge and gasped in horror as he saw his brother desperately trying to climb up the long, swaying rope.

"Hold on, Morton!" cried Warton. "Hold on!"

Immediately, he began tugging on the rope. He pulled with all his strength, and as the long rope began to pile up ever so slowly at his feet it seemed to him that time had come to a stop. At last there appeared, staring over the edge of the old washtub, the most frightened-looking face imaginable. Warton quickly grabbed hold of his brother and yanked hard, and the two toads plopped onto the floor.

For several moments Warton and Morton could only stare at each other. Then they crawled to one side of the tub and peered over the edge. They both groaned as they saw the treetops passing swiftly beneath them.

"Quick!" cried Morton. "What must we do to make this contraption go down?"

Warton looked sadly at his brother. "There is no way," he said. "I'm afraid we'll have to go wherever the wind takes us."

Morton gulped.

The two toads looked longingly back at the vanishing hillside and the giant twin hemlock that stood above their home. They watched till the hillside was gone, and the hemlock disappeared among the countless trees of the forest.

His eyes dark with concern, Warton turned around. "Morton!" he cried out in alarm. "Look where the wind is taking us!"

Morton turned, and his knees buckled as he saw their destination.

The little craft was being swept straight towards the red cliffs—the same red cliffs where the two toads had once seen the hungry hawks soaring round and round in endless circles as they searched for hapless victims to pounce upon and then to devour.

As *The King of the Skies* drifted along, the sunlight falling on the snakeskins made their soft colors glow, and it seemed as if a beautiful, delicate balloon were floating serenely over the forest.

On the craft itself, however, things were far from serene. Warton was furiously pulling on the ropes attached to the snakeskins, hoping that somehow it would change their direction of travel. At the same time Morton was searching the skies above and the forest below, keeping a constant watch for any signs of the dreaded hawks.

At last Warton let loose of the ropes. "It's no use," he said. "Our only hope is that the wind will change."

"I'm afraid it is changing," said Morton. "Listen!"

A low whistling sound was coming from the snakeskin tubes overhead. With a sinking heart

27

Warton realized it was caused by the high winds, which had started blowing much harder. The little craft was being whisked ever faster over the tree-tops, but still in the same direction.

Soon the towering red cliffs, which to Warton and Morton had always seemed so distant and mysterious, were directly before them. There could be no doubt that the little balloon was soon to end its voyage with a crashing stop against their rocky walls.

Warton looked at his brother. "I'm sorry it turned out this way, Morton," he said. "I only wanted to make a surprise for you."

"Never mind that," said Morton. "Just curl yourself into a tight ball. It may help when we hit."

"Right," replied Warton. "And good luck!"

There was no time for anything else. *The King of the Skies,* the paint on its sides not yet dry, crashed against the stone wall of the cliff.

Warton heard the boards of the tub scrape and splinter. Overhead he heard the tearing and ripping of the snakeskins. He felt a sudden jolt and

everything seemed to shudder. He took a deep breath and prepared to crash to earth like a falling stone. But to his great surprise, because of the strong winds that always swept up from the bottom of the cliff, the balloon wobbled a bit then, like a dry leaf in autumn, fluttered slowly downward till it came to rest on solid ground.

All was silent. Warton let out the big puff of air he had been holding in and looked about. For a moment he was unable to see a thing. Red dust, scraped off the side of the cliff, swirled all around. When it settled a bit he was shocked to see that Morton was still lying on the floor of the tub, curled up like a ball, his eyes wide and staring.

"Morton!" cried Warton. "Speak to me!"

Morton blinked. Then, moving only his eyes, he looked straight at Warton. "Very ... well," he said slowly. "Please ... promise ... never ... to ... make ... a ... surprise ... for ... me ... again!"

Warton was overjoyed that his brother was all right. "I promise," he said.

"Thank you," replied Morton. "Now, let's see if we are still in one piece."

The two toads stood, brushed off the red dust as best they could, and climbed out of the shattered tub. As they caught their breath they looked about.

"We're on the edge of a hollow," said Warton. "There's a stream down there running through the middle of it."

"I know," said Morton. "I noticed it when we were up in the air. That's the same stream that runs past our home."

"It is?" said Warton. "Why, that's wonderful.

That means all we have to do is follow it, and we won't have to worry about getting lost. We'll be home in no time!"

Morton was shaking his head. "It may not be that simple," he said. "You forget, we won't be traveling *over* the forest this time—we'll be traveling *through* it. We'll be afoot in places that are completely unfamiliar to us. There could be many dangers, and we must go very carefully each step of the way. It may be several days before we see our home again."

Warton, realizing the truth in what his brother said, began to frown. His eyes turned towards the little meadow that lay before them. Suddenly he blinked. The frown vanished and a smile appeared in its place. "Perhaps it won't take us long to return home after all," he said. "I've got an idea!"

"Oh, no!" cried Morton. "I refuse to go up in the air again!"

"You won't have to," said Warton. "This time we can go on the water."

Morton looked quizzically at his brother. "Water?" he said.

"Right," said Warton. "Look, I have my carpenter tools right here in my belt. I can easily fix the washtub. Then we could put it in that stream, and we'll float all the way home."

Morton looked at Warton. Suddenly his face brightened. "I must say," he said, "that's not a bad idea. I'm sure it would be the safest way to travel."

"And fastest," said Warton. "But we'd better hurry before a hawk sees us."

Quickly the toads unfastened the snakeskin tubes. Then, each taking a side of the tub, they started for the stream.

"Just think how lucky we are," said Warton as they walked down into the hollow. "We're safely back on the ground, and after a little ride down that stream, we'll soon be home, and neither of us harmed in any way."

"I hope you're right," said Morton, glancing nervously up at the sky. "But I won't feel safe till we're far away from these cliffs."

As they got deeper into the hollow they could see that the stream had its beginning at the bottom of the cliff. Then it twisted and turned through scattered white birches. The grass that grew up to its edges was thick and dark green. Yellow and purple wildflowers grew everywhere, and the air smelled sweet. It was a glorious scene, and there was not a hawk in sight.

Yet, as they went ever deeper into the hollow, Warton noticed that he was beginning to feel a bit uneasy. He turned to Morton. "Have you noticed how quiet it is here?" he said.

"I certainly have," replied Morton. "I haven't seen a mouse or a rabbit or a squirrel, and I haven't heard a single note from a bird of any kind."

As they went farther along, Warton found that his uneasy feeling was growing ever stronger.

At last they came to the stream, and Warton spotted a place where the water rippled onto a sandy beach. "I'll fix the tub down there," he said.

"And I'll go look for something to waterproof it," said Morton, "and a long pole to push with."

Warton dragged the tub down to the beach and immediately began repairing it. Morton returned quickly with some thick, gooey pine pitch, and then he went off to look for a pole. Using the pitch and a few pieces of driftwood that lay nearby, it wasn't long before Warton had the tub as good as new. He took a drink of the clear water and sat down on the warm sand to wait for Morton. As he looked about he wondered why such a beautiful, peaceful place should hold no signs of life.

And then he heard the first sound he had heard since the balloon had landed. A shrill and angry bark came from somewhere beyond the stream bank. Then Morton's voice carried to him, loud and clear. "Run, Warton! Run!"

Instantly Warton jumped up. He leaped up onto the bank, and saw two animals slinking towards Morton. At first they looked like harmless squirrels, but Warton quickly realized that these creatures were far from harmless. The low slung bodies with the rich brown fur on the backs and the pure white fur on the bellies, the short powerful legs, the pointed teeth, and the shiny dark eyes meant only one thing—these were the most bloodthirsty and ferocious animals of the whole forest.

"Weasels!" cried Warton.

"Get him!" commanded a sharp voice.

Warton spun around and saw two more weasels. They crept slowly towards him. Their tails were straight out, the muscles in their strong legs were tight, and their black eyes were shining.

Warton tried to get to Morton's side. But as soon as he took one step, the weasel farthest away moved, and with lightning speed appeared directly in front of him. Face to face with the fero-

cious creature, Warton felt a chill run through him. He noticed the drops of dried blood that stained the weasel's pointy chin.

Warton could see no way of escape.

Then the weasel flicked his tail.

Warton squeezed his eyes shut and waited for him to pounce.

"Follow me!" commanded the weasel.

Warton was stunned. He blinked and then looked over at Morton, noticing with relief that he too was still all right.

"Well," snarled the plumpest weasel, whose belly nearly touched the ground, "you heard what Fulton said. Let's go!"

Warton had no more time to wonder what was happening. He followed along behind the fat weasel, while Morton fell behind one of the others. They walked beside the grassy stream bank till they came to a lightly wooded area. The weasels made their way through the trees and around several boulders, and stopped when they came to an overturned pine. Under its snarled and twisted roots Warton saw a dark hole.

"In there!" said the fat weasel.

Warton entered, and, feeling the solid earth under him, he knew it had taken many feet to pack it so hard. The hole went sharply downward, then turned and stopped before a flat stone.

"Wait," said the weasel called Fulton. He put his weight against the stone and easily moved it aside.

Warton stepped through another smaller hole and found himself standing in a large room with a ceiling made of stone and walls that were part dirt and part wood. Pieces of pine tree roots poked out in several places. When Warton looked at the floor he shivered, for it was covered from wall to wall with furs. There were squirrel, rabbit, chipmunk, skunk, and many others. Quickly he looked away, and then he noticed a long table that stood in the middle of the room. Four chairs were along each side and one at either end.

As soon as they were all inside, Warton turned towards the weasel called Fulton. "Why have you brought us here?" he asked in a trembling voice.

Without even looking at Warton, Fulton strolled across the room. "Tell him, Fritz," he called as he disappeared into one of two passageways.

Fritz, the weasel with the big belly, was curling up in a corner of the room. "I'm too tired," he said with a yawn. "You tell him, Fred."

"I don't have to tell him anything," grumbled one of the weasels. "You tell him, Floyd," and Fred started to walk away.

"I don't want to," said Floyd. "It's too much bother."

At that, Fred spun around and put his face directly in front of Floyd's. "Everything's too much bother for you," he snarled, and he began clicking his sharp teeth at Floyd.

That seemed to annoy Floyd very much, and he gave Fred a hard shove. Fred instantly shoved back, and the two fell to wrestling. They rolled

over and over on the floor, poking and snapping at each other till they were both exhausted. Then they separated, and each lay down and shut his eyes.

The weasels quickly fell asleep, and then Warton realized no one was watching him and Morton. "Morton," he whispered, "this is our chance. We may be able to sneak out of here before they wake up!"

"I was thinking the same thing," said Morton.

They started for the hole they had just come through.

"Oh, oh," said Warton, "they've rolled the stone back!"

The two toads pushed hard, but it was far too heavy for them to budge.

"We'd better look for another way out," said Morton.

Quickly they stole past the long table. At the other end of the room they stood before the two passageways. Warton stepped into the first, and Morton followed. They saw a room on each side, and one at the end of the passageway. Peeking in the first room they saw two weasels curled up and sleeping soundly. Cautiously, they went on to the second room.

Warton was the first to look in. "It's filled with

garbage and junk," he whispered. "No way out here."

The two toads hurried along the passageway till they came to the room at the end. They heard quite a bit of clattering and banging going on inside, and someone singing in a very off-key voice. Ever so carefully, Warton and Morton peered in from each side of the doorway.

"It's their kitchen!" said Warton, his eyes wide.

"It's horrible!" gasped Morton.

The counter was piled high with dirty pots and pans, and the sink overflowed with filthy dishes. There were stains on the ceiling, spots on the walls, and spills on the floor. A big stove was completely covered with bits of old food.

"It's the most disgusting kitchen I've ever seen," whispered Morton.

Then a cupboard door slammed shut and the two toads saw a weasel about half the size of the others standing before a counter. She was wearing a huge blue bow on her head, and as she filled a jar with peppercorns, she sang loudly in a hoarse voice.

"We'd better get away before she sees us," said Warton.

"The sooner the better," said Morton. "I hope I never see such a sight again."

They hurried back to the big room and, finding the weasels still asleep, entered the other passageway. They saw only a single room along one side, but at the far end they noticed the passageway turned a corner, and they headed there.

Just as they reached the bend, they came face to face with Fulton.

"Looking for a way out?" he laughed. "Well, look all you want, because there's only one—the way you came in."

Dejectedly, Warton and Morton turned around

and went back to the big room, with Fulton right behind them. The moment they entered the room, the weasel they had seen in the kitchen stepped out of the other passageway, carrying a large platter filled with buns.

"Supper's ready!" she shouted at the top of her voice.

Immediately, Floyd, Fred, and Fritz jumped to their feet. The two weasels who had been sleeping in the first room came dashing out. Two other weasels charged out of the second passageway. They shoved, pushed, and fell all over one another in their haste to get to the long table.

When everyone was seated, the smaller weasel set the platter in the middle of the table alongside a pitcher filled with a rosy liquid.

"Oh, no, Freda," groaned one of the weasels, "not ratburgers again."

Freda gave him a steely-eyed look. "If you don't like them, Felix," she snapped, "*you* can do the cooking around here!"

Felix managed a small smile. "I like them," he said meekly. And he reached for two of the burgers. "And I believe I'd like some of your delicious rhubarb cider, too," he said, filling his mug from the pitcher.

The other weasels jostled and jabbed and poked and punched as they grabbed for the burgers and cider. The noise in the room was soon so loud, it made the pine roots sticking out of the walls actually quiver. All the weasels argued and talked at once. Then Fred and Fritz tried seeing who could sing the highest note. Floyd started to whistle, but his mouth was so full he sprayed bits of food all over Freda. Freda let out a shout and smacked him hard with a ratburger.

All the while, Warton and Morton watched in silence, shocked by the weasels' behavior.

Then Fulton stood up on his chair and let out the loudest yell Warton had ever heard. "Shut up, everybody!" He yelled five times before the room finally grew quieter. "You all know it's my turn to be leader this week. Now, listen to me!"

"Oh, all right," said Felix. "What is it?"

"Well," said Fulton, glad to be getting some attention, "have you all noticed the toads Fritz, Fred, Floyd, and I captured today?"

All eyes turned towards Warton and Morton standing in the middle of the room.

"Of course we noticed," said the weasel next to Fulton, "and I say let's eat them now."

Fulton turned and shoved him right out of his chair. "Too bad you don't use your brain once in a while like I do, Frank, because then you'd have a much better idea."

"And just what is your wonderful idea?" said a weasel with hardly any hair on his tail.

Fulton looked slowly around the table. "Well," he said importantly, "isn't it true that, since the tree we live under blew over, we've needed a new home badly?"

"That's true," grumbled Fred, "especially when it rains."

"I'd give anything for a room of my own," said Fritz.

"Anyone as fat as you needs *two* rooms," snickered Floyd.

At that, Fritz stamped down hard on Floyd's foot. Floyd let out a yowl and started hopping around the table in agony, while Fritz laughed loudly.

Fulton paid them no attention. "And isn't it

true," he said, "that we've tried to build a new home many times?"

"You know very well it's true, you big windbag," said a weasel with a pure white head.

"Good for you, Francis," chuckled the weasel next to him. "Now ask him *why* we haven't done it yet."

Before Fulton could say any more, there was a loud banging at the far end of the table. Freda, who had been hitting her mug against the table, stood up on her chair. Her cheeks bulged out with food. Her blue bow dangled loosely on one side of her head. "I'll tell you why, Farley, and the rest of you too," she mumbled. "It's because you're all uncivilized ... and you're unruly ... and ... " She paused to take several huge swallows from her mug. Then, as rhubarb cider dribbled down her chin, she went on. "You're all so disgusting it makes me ashamed to admit that I'm your sister." Freda snatched another burger, sat down, and the room was quiet.

"Well, she's right about that," said Floyd.

"It's the truth," said Farley.

"So what!" said Fred. "It's nothing new."

"I guess we'll *never* have a new home," said Frank.

Fulton looked disdainfully at Frank and knocked him out of his chair again. "Didn't I tell you I have a good idea?"

"Well, what is it?" gasped Frank from the floor.

Fulton turned and pointed straight at Warton. "When I saw that toad today and what he was wearing, I knew it could mean only one thing!"

Warton suddenly realized he still had on his tool belt and carpenter's hat.

"And what it means," said Fulton proudly, "is that that toad must be some kind of a construction expert, and that other one is his assistant. Therefore, with an expert to show us what to do, we'll have a new home by tomorrow night."

Suddenly, all the weasels grew greatly excited. They whistled and clapped and stomped their feet.

"Wait!" shouted Floyd. "What if even they can't help us?"

"That's simple," said Fred. "Then we'll have two more furs for our floor."

Floyd put his nose directly against Fred's. "And how, may I ask, does one get fur off a toad?"

Fred looked a bit embarrassed as he realized his mistake. "Well," he said slowly, "maybe we could make vests out of them."

"Now, that's the first sensible thing you've said today," said Floyd.

Warton could keep quiet no longer. "But I'm not a construction expert," he cried.

"And I'm not an assistant," spoke up Morton.

Fulton and the other weasels laughed loudly. "You can't fool us," said Fulton. "So remember this—tomorrow you are to show us how to build a

new home. If you don't, you'll never see your own home again. In the meantime, you can eat our food and you can sleep in the garbage and junk room."

Freda got out of her chair and stood in front of Morton. "And as long as you are an assistant," she said, "you can help me in my kitchen tomorrow." She whirled around and left the room.

As once again the weasels started shouting, pushing, and wrestling among themselves, Warton and Morton looked helplessly at each other.

"We're in terrible trouble," said Morton. "We must do something quickly!"

"I know," agreed Warton.

The two toads decided to go to the room where Fulton said they could sleep. Perhaps there, where there was less commotion, they might think better about what to do.

Warton was just entering the passageway when Morton shouted, "Wait!" He hopped to the long table, grabbed two burgers, and hurried back to Warton. "No matter what happens," he said as they went along the tunnel, "we must always remember to eat to keep up our strength."

As soon as they stepped into the garbage and junk room, they began digging into the mess. When they were done, they had completely cleared a small place in one corner. Then they found an old crate to serve as a table, a broken stool, and a wooden bucket to sit on. After that they each made a small bed out of old rags. Satisfied at last that it was as livable as they could make it, they ate the ratburgers, which neither toad cared for very much.

Then they sat on the floor with their backs against the wall and tried to think about what to do next. As Warton stared at the ceiling and Morton stared at the floor, they could hear a constant commotion coming from the big room as the brawling weasels carried on their arguing and tumbling about. But in the garbage and junk room not a sound was made.

At last Warton let out a long sigh. "I'm afraid I can think of no way to convince those weasels we are not what they think we are," he said glumly.

There was another long silence. Then Morton spoke. "Perhaps we shouldn't," he said. "After all, it's the only reason we are still alive."

Warton blinked. "But then I would have to pretend to be a construction expert tomorrow, and you an assistant."

Morton nodded.

"But...but I'm not," cried Warton, "and you're not!"

"I know," said Morton, his face solemn. "But you have built many things, and with your ingenuity I wouldn't be at all surprised if you could help those weasels. And from the looks of Freda's kitchen, I'm sure I can do whatever assisting she should ask for."

Warton was aghast. "But ... but I don't even know how a construction expert should act."

"They act with authority," said Morton. "I'm sure of that. And they always take charge."

"T...T...Take charge?" stammered Warton as he thought of the eight wild weasels brawling and shouting out in the big room. Then he looked at Morton. He gulped hard. "Very well," he said. "I know it's the only thing we can do, so tomorrow I'll do my best to act like a construction expert."

"And I will do my best to help Freda in her kitchen." Morton choked as he said it.

By then it was late, and both toads were extremely tired. They curled up on their beds of rags, and quickly went to sleep.

Warton was still tired the next morning, but he got right up. "Those weasels must be anxious to get started," he said.

"I wish I could go with you," said Morton as he got up too. "Instead, I must help Freda in that terrible kitchen."

"Well, it's only for one day," said Warton. Then he gulped as he realized what would happen if the weasels didn't get their home built.

Out in the passageway, Morton whispered to Warton, "Now remember, you must act with authority and take command." Then he started for the kitchen.

Warton sighed and, with a heavy heart, turned towards the big room. When he got there, he was surprised to find no one waiting for him at all. There were two weasels there, but they were sound asleep. Fred was curled up in a corner, and Fritz was stretched out on the table.

Warton sat down. He waited and waited, but no one moved, and there wasn't a sound anywhere.

"They'll never get their new home if they don't start soon—the morning is half gone already." As Warton said this to himself, he realized he was still wearing the little whistle around his neck, and recalled the last thing Morton had said to him. "Hmmm," he said, "I wonder if I dare?" He hesitated a moment longer, then he said, "I must!" He took a deep breath, put the whistle to his mouth, and blew as hard as he could.

Fred instantly sprang to his feet. Fritz was so startled he rolled off the table.

"About time you woke up," said Warton, trying not to sound nervous. "Now, wait here while I wake the others." Soon, loud blasts of the whistle filled the weasels' home, and Warton could be heard shouting, "Wake up, you weasels! It's time to go to work!"

Very confused and startled weasels began pouring into the big room.

"Where is that toad?" said Floyd as he staggered in. "I'm going to eat him right now!"

"No!" cried Fulton. "We'll never get a new home if you do!"

Floyd growled, but followed after the others as they started for the hole that went outdoors.

Just then, Morton stepped out of a passageway. His sleeves were rolled up and he had a towel wrapped around his stomach. "Aren't you going to eat breakfast?" he asked.

"No," growled Fred. "We only eat supper."

Morton appeared shocked. He looked at the weasels, who were all ready to leave. "Well, I'm sorry," he said, "but if there is one thing my brother always insists on before he starts a hard day of construction work, it's a hearty breakfast. Isn't that right, Warton?"

For a moment, Warton was taken aback. But then he said, "Oh, yes, that's right. I always say, lots of good food means lots of good work."

"Then follow me," said Morton, and he started back to the kitchen. "I'll have something ready in a jiffy."

The weasels stared flabbergasted at each other as Warton followed after Morton.

In the kitchen, Warton noticed that Freda was lying under the sink. Three flies were buzzing around her head as she slept. Morton poked through the cluttered cupboards till he found what he needed to make four big pancakes. He fried them as quickly as he could on the dirty stove, muttering, "Disgusting, disgusting, disgusting." Warton watched from a stool nearby.

As Warton and Morton ate, Freda awoke.

"What's going on?" she demanded. "This is my kitchen."

"I made us a small breakfast," replied Morton. "I hope you don't mind."

"Well," said Freda with a yawn. "See that you don't leave a mess." And she went back to sleep.

Morton nearly choked.

When Warton returned to the big room, three of the weasels were wrestling, Fred and Floyd were arguing about who could stand on one foot the longest, and the others had gone to sleep.

Warton gave a loud blast on his whistle and found he was beginning to enjoy it a bit. "All right, weasels," he shouted, "let's not waste any more time!"

Fred growled, puffed out his cheeks, and charged at Warton. Fulton stopped him just in time and spun him around towards the doorway.

One by one, the weasels filed up the tunnel. Outside, Fulton led the way and, before long, they came to a place where a fallen log lay across the stream. Fulton started across first, with Warton just behind him. As they reached the other side,

Warton heard a plop. He turned around and saw
Fred splashing about in the water. Floyd was
standing on the log with a big grin on his face.
Suddenly Fritz got a mischievous look and gave
Floyd a shove. Then Frank pushed Fritz, and Felix
pushed Francis. And, in a few moments, all the
weasels were in the water trying to drown each
other.

Finally, they staggered onto the grass, where
Warton was waiting. They stayed there for some
time shouting and accusing each other of being the
worst weasel ever born. It was nearly noon when, at
last, they quieted down and Fulton led the way
once again. They went on till they came to a big
pine tree on a little hill by the stream. Sticking out
of the earth below the tree was a flat rock.

"Our new home is to be under that rock," said Fulton. "It was used by rabbits once. There are plenty of tunnels and rooms in there, but it needs to be cleaned out and made bigger."

Hope stirred in Warton's heart. "Why, that doesn't seem like much of a job," he thought. "Especially with eight strong weasels to do the work." As he stood there staring at the rabbit hole, he suddenly realized that all eyes were upon him.

"Well," he said clearing his throat, "the first thing I must do is look the situation over." He took out his folding ruler and strode towards the flat rock. Stopping just outside the entrance, he carefully measured the hole from top to bottom. "Hmmm," he said thoughtfully. Then he measured the hole from side to side. "Ah ha!" he said, and he gave his ruler a tap.

As the weasels watched, Warton stepped inside. He quickly looked about, and with great relief saw that everything was dry and seemed quite sound. "This will be even easier than I thought," he said to himself with a smile. "And, for the life of me, I can't see why they should need any help at all."

Then, trying to look very stern, he stepped back outside. He blew a blast on his whistle. "All right, weasels," he shouted in his most commanding voice, "come get your orders!"

"I'm going to finish him off this minute," snarled Floyd. But Fritz and Frank held him back. Then the weasels walked slowly towards Warton.

"First of all," said Warton, "everyone will have to do a certain job. Now, who wants to dig?"

"I'm not digging," said Felix. "I hate to dig."

"I suppose you want me to dig for you," snapped Fred. He clicked his teeth in front of Felix. Without a moment's delay, Felix gave Fred a push. Fred fell on Frank. And, once again, weasels were shouting and grabbing at each other as they rolled about on the hillside.

Warton watched helplessly, until they finally

63

quieted down, and lay huffing and puffing. He took a deep breath and said, "Well, who's ready for work?"

"Not me," said Fred, "I'm too tired. I've got to rest."

"Me too," said Fritz as he stretched out and shut his eyes.

Warton shook his head.

It was mid-afternoon when the weasels said they were rested enough to go to work. Frank and Floyd finally agreed that they would both dig. Felix and Fritz said they would carry the dirt out. And Fulton, Fred, Francis, and Farley said they would gnaw off roots and roll away stones.

As the weasels disappeared under the rock into the hillside, Warton sighed with relief. "Perhaps," he thought, "with my idea of assigning certain tasks, the weasels *will* have a new home. Then Morton and I can go to our own home."

Warton was beginning to feel somewhat better, and began to hum a little tune. Suddenly, a great roar came from the new home. Warton spun around and saw Fred come running out.

Floyd was right behind him shouting, "I'll teach you to bite my tail!"

"I thought it was a root," wailed Fred.

Then Frank came tearing out. Hobbling after him was Fritz. "You dropped that rock on my foot on purpose!" he cried.

"It was an accident," giggled Frank as he ran behind a tree.

Other weasels were running out now. They were arguing and shouting. Then they started pushing and shoving.

Warton watched the weasels scrambling all over the hillside, and his face grew as long as the afternoon shadows.

It was a long time before the squabbling stopped. Then the weasels were too tired to work. In desperation Warton went inside, and carried out several small piles of dirt himself. He pushed at stones and broke off roots. But it was far too much for him. Finally, exhausted and dirty, he stepped back outside. The weasels were still lying about and, with eyes full of despair, Warton noticed the sun was beginning to set.

Then Fulton stood up. "I guess even a construction expert can't help *us*," he said. "Let's go home."

Warton swallowed hard and fell in line with the weasels. He dragged his weary feet down the hill, across the log, through the woods, and then down the tunnel and once again into the big room of the weasels' old home.

Freda was just putting a large bowl on the table. Morton was setting a platter beside it. When he heard the weasels come in, he looked towards Warton, high hopes showing all over his face.

"Well, Freda," said Floyd, "we still don't have a new home, so you'd better get ready to cook these toads for supper."

Morton's mouth dropped.

"Listen, stupid," said Freda, "I've already got supper made. We can have the toads tomorrow night. Tonight we're having shrew stew. Take it or leave it!" She left in a huff.

As the weasels scattered about, Morton went to Warton's side. "I'm sure you did all you could," he said. "One day just wasn't enough time."

Warton shook his head. "One hundred days wouldn't be enough time," he said. "It's just impossible for those weasels to work together."

Freda returned from the kitchen and set a pitcher of pumpkin punch on the table. "Supper's ready!" she shouted.

Immediately the weasels began climbing all over each other as they rushed to their seats.

"Hey!" shouted Frank. "The toads should eat too. We want them to stay plump till tomorrow!"

Morton looked at Warton. "I suppose we should to keep up our strength," he said, "even to the very end."

The toads sat together in the empty end chair. The weasels ate in their usual rough and tumble way, each trying to get whatever he could for himself. They scooped out the stew without bothering to use spoons, and filled their bowls till they overflowed. It was all Warton and Morton could do to get half a bowl, which they shared.

"It's really not bad," said Warton after the first taste.

"Needs salt," grunted Morton.

They were still eating when Freda stood on her chair, the other weasels having already finished the very last morsel of stew. "Tonight," screeched Freda, "we're having something new that my assistant told me about. It's called dessert."

"Dessert?" said Fred. "What's dessert?"

"It's something you eat after you've finished eating," said Freda. "The toad made it himself."

"They're my special wintergreen and raspberry cookies," whispered Morton to Warton.

"Well, if dessert means more food," said Fritz, "I'm for it." He reached for a red cookie. "Hmmm," he said, "not bad."

"Is that so?" said Frank. "Then let me have one."

"Sure," said Fritz, and he hurled a green one at Frank.

Floyd immediately threw one at Francis.

Cookies began sailing across the table in all directions, filling the air, and Morton watched sadly

as they smashed against the walls. Finally, he got up, trudged across the room, and entered the passageway that led to the garbage and junk room. Warton trudged after him.

When Warton stepped inside, he found Morton lying on his pile of rags staring up at the ceiling. As Warton looked at him, he realized that, not once, had Morton complained about the predicament they were in. And he wished with all his heart that there was some way he could cheer his brother up.

Warton told a little joke and hoped Morton

would laugh. But Morton couldn't even smile.

"How about singing a couple of songs?" said Warton.

Morton shook his head.

Warton knew he must do something. His eyes began to blink. They blinked faster and faster, and, when they stopped, he started poking about the messy room. When he found an old piece of board, he drew several lines on it with a chunk of charcoal. Then he went into the big room.

The weasels, who were either sleeping or arguing or wrestling, paid Warton no attention, and he went along the walls picking up pieces of red and green cookies till he had twenty-four of them. Then he hurried back to the garbage and junk room.

Morton was still lying on the rags, his eyes shut.

Warton stood over him. "Care for a game of checkers?"

Morton's eyes popped open. "Why..." he said, seeing Warton's newly made checkerboard, "that would be very nice."

"Okay," said Warton. "And I'll be green if you

don't mind." He began to arrange the cookie pieces on the checkerboard.

Before half of the first game was over, Warton could see the gloominess vanish from Morton's face. They were just starting their third game when Fred came in with a load of garbage. He threw the garbage on a pile and went over to Warton and Morton.

"What are you doing?" he demanded.

"We're playing checkers," replied Warton.

"Oh," said Fred. "What's checkers?"

"It's a game," said Morton.

"Oh," said Fred. "What's a game?"

Warton and Morton looked at Fred in amazement.

"Don't you know what a game is?" asked Warton.

"No," said Fred. "I can't know everything."

"Well," said Morton, "it's a bit hard to explain."

"Then show me," said Fred, pulling up a box and sitting down beside Warton.

The toads could see that Fred would not be satisfied till he knew what the game of checkers was. So Warton let Fred use the green cookies, and Morton played against him with the red cookies. Warton and Morton explained some of the simplest facts about checkers as they played. The game was over very quickly and Morton won easily.

"Now, do you understand?" said Morton.

"Not yet," said Fred. "Let's play another game."

"All right," said Morton, and they started playing again.

Morton won that game too, but this time it was much closer. Morton could see that Fred was a fast learner, and seemed to enjoy the game immensely.

"Let's play again," said Fred.

"All right," agreed Morton, and he and Fred

played four more games. By then it was growing late. Morton had all he could do to keep his eyes open. "I'm sorry," he said with a big yawn, "but I'm just too tired to play anymore."

"Oh," said Fred with disappointment. "Well, then I'll just take this game into the big room and play checkers with someone else."

As Fred left, Morton lay down on his pile of rags. "Goodnight, Warton," he said as he shut his eyes, "and thank you for thinking of the checkers."

"Goodnight," said Warton, happy that he had been able to take Morton's mind off their terrible problem for at least a little while.

The two toads had been asleep a short time when Fred came tearing into the room. Floyd was right behind him. "Wake up!" shouted Fred.

"What's wrong?" asked Warton and Morton together.

"I don't know," said Fred, waving the checker-board in the air. "When I played this game with you it was fun. I want to know why it wasn't fun when I played with Floyd."

"It's because you wouldn't let me have red," said Floyd.

"I say it's because you wouldn't let me go first," said Fred.

"And I say this game is impossible," said Floyd, giving Fred a shove.

In an instant, the two weasels were fighting. They rolled through the garbage and junk till they were all tired out. Then they sat glaring at each other.

Finally, Fred pointed at Warton and Morton. "You two play," he demanded.

Warton spread out the checkerboard. "Red or green?" he said to Morton, and the two sleepy toads played checkers.

Every once in a while Fred poked Floyd and said, "See?"

Floyd seemed fascinated. As soon as the game was over, he grabbed the checkerboard and ran out of the room with Fred chasing after him.

When the weasels had gone, Warton and Morton just shook their heads and went back to sleep.

Warton did not sleep well that night at all. He tossed and turned and had many bad dreams about what was going to happen the next day. Very early in the morning, he got out of his rag bed. Seeing that Morton was still asleep, he carefully made his way through the junk.

"Now," he said to himself when he was out of the room, "I'm going to search that other passageway just in case Fulton was not telling the truth about another way out."

He tiptoed along the tunnel, being very careful not to wake the weasels. At the entrance to the big room he glanced behind him, then stepped in.

Warton blinked. Except for Freda, every weasel was there. Fred and Floyd were at one end of the table. Fritz and Fulton were at the other end. Farley and Francis sat across from each other at the middle of the table, and in a corner of the room Frank and Felix were sitting on the floor.

As shocked as Warton was at seeing all the weasels there, he was even more shocked by the way they were behaving. He could see they were wide awake and yet... they weren't arguing, they weren't shouting, and they weren't wrestling. They weren't making a sound. Each weasel seemed to be concentrating all his thoughts on something that lay before him.

It was too much for Warton's curiosity. He stepped closer and closer and then... when he saw what they were doing, he could hardly believe his eyes. "Checkers!" he gasped. "They're all playing checkers!"

Warton noticed his own checkerboard being used by Fred and Floyd. The others, he could see, had made boards just like it. "And it looks to me," he said aloud, "like they've been playing all night!"

He whirled around and dashed back to the garbage and junk room. "Come quick!" he said, shaking his slumbering brother.

"Oh no!" cried Morton. "Our time has come!"

"Not yet," said Warton. "And maybe it won't. Hurry!"

When Morton saw what the weasels were doing he was astonished. "I can't believe it," he said. "This is the first time they haven't been fighting and arguing."

"I know," said Warton, "and it's given me an idea."

Before Morton could ask what it was, Warton hopped over to the table. "I see you enjoy playing checkers," he said to Fulton.

"Don't bother me," grumbled the weasel. "Can't you see I'm trying to figure out my next move?"

Warton went right on. "Checkers is fun, all

right," he said loudly. "Of course, it isn't as much fun as . . . volleyball."

Fulton froze. Fred's head snapped up. Every weasel stared at Warton.

"Do you mean there's another game besides checkers?" said Fulton.

"Oh, yes," said Warton. "But I don't think weasels could play it." He turned and winked at Morton.

"Is that so!" said Fulton indignantly. "Well, you'd better show us how to play that game right now!"

"Oh, all right," said Warton. "If you insist."

It didn't take Warton long to fashion a ball from two lizard skins he had seen in the garbage and junk room. As soon as Fritz blew it up, he plugged the little hole with a gob of pine pitch.

"First," said Warton, "we must go outdoors."

The weasels eagerly followed Warton and Morton to a grassy clearing down by the stream. There Warton strung a rope between two saplings.

"Next," he said, "we need two teams."

"What's a team?" demanded Floyd.

"A team will be four weasels," said Warton, "who will play together and help each other in order to beat the other team of four weasels."

The weasels looked disgusted at the thought of helping each other, but, after much grumbling, they decided that Fred, Floyd, Felix, and Francis would be on one team, and Fulton, Fritz, Frank and Farley would be on the other.

"Now," said Warton, "each team has to keep the ball from landing on their side of the rope."

"Simple," said Fulton.

"Let's get started," said Frank.

Warton blew his whistle and stepped back beside Morton to watch. "After they learn teamwork," he whispered, "it will be a simple matter for them to build their new home."

"I hope you're right," said Morton, looking worried.

Very shortly, a great deal of shouting came from the volleyball players. The weasels were all glaring at Fritz, who was sitting on the ball. "I should hit the ball more often," he complained. "I blew it up, didn't I?"

"I was the closest," shouted Frank. "I should hit it."

"I'd like to hit them both," cried Fred.

Warton and Morton held their breath, and somehow the weasels started playing again.

In a little while, though, a commotion began once more. This time Francis was pointing accusingly at Felix. "You shoved me on purpose," he yelled, and gave Felix a hard push. In an instant, all the weasels were wrestling with one another.

Warton watched in dismay as they rolled about in the grass. With a saddened face he sat down on a rock beside Morton. "It's no use," he said dejectedly. "They can never do anything together ... never."

At that moment, Freda appeared at the edge of the grassy clearing. Her apron flapping in the breeze, she shouted to the weasels, "I'm ready to start supper. What's it to be?"

One by one, the weasels stood up and began moving towards the toads.

Warton gulped and Morton began to shake.

Just then, a dark shadow crept across the grass.

A horrifying shriek came from overhead, and a hawk plunged out of the sky. With its claws spread wide, it dropped downwards. Then, with dazzling speed, it turned at the edge of the clearing and shot back up into the air. And Freda was gone!

It happened so quickly, everyone was stunned,

and they watched speechless as the hawk flew towards the red cliffs. When it reached its nest high on the sheer wall, the hawk dropped Freda into it, then made a circle and sailed off.

"Look!" cried Fulton. "He's gone to hunt somewhere else!"

"If Freda can only get down before he comes back," said Fritz.

Frank gave him a poke. "I suppose you think she can fly!" he said.

"I know she can't fly," said Fritz. "But it would be nice if she could."

Warton's eyes were darting back and forth. First to the cliffs, then to the weasels, then to Morton, and then back to the cliffs. Suddenly, he had to speak up. *The King of the Skies* can fly!" he exclaimed.

The weasels stared at him.

Fulton put his pointy chin against Warton's nose. "And *who* is the king of the skies?" he snarled.

Warton swallowed. "It's the balloon my brother and I flew here in. It's all apart now, but if it were put back together before the hawk comes back, Freda could come down in it."

The weasels looked at each other.

"I think it's a trick," said Floyd.

"Sure it is," agreed Frank. "Why would they want to help us?"

Fulton looked thoughtful. "It probably is," he said. He thought some more. "But does anyone have a better idea?"

No one answered.

"All right then," said Fulton, glaring at Warton, "put that balloon back together fast."

"I'll need my tool belt that's back in the garbage and junk room," said Warton.

"Don't forget the tub," said Morton. "It must still be by the stream where we were captured."

"And the snakeskin tubes," said Warton. "They're at the bottom of the cliffs, but I don't know where exactly."

"I'll get the tool belt," said Felix, and he dashed off towards home.

Fred and Floyd were already running towards the stream.

"Meet us under the hawk's nest," said Fulton to Fritz, "and make sure those toads don't run away. The rest of us will look for the snakeskin tubes, whatever they are."

Warton and Morton, following after Fritz, hurried along as fast as they could. When they reached the cliffs, the weasels were all there, waiting impatiently.

Right away, Warton and Morton set to work sewing up the holes and tears that were in the tubes. As soon as they were finished, Fred, Frank, and Felix helped Warton fasten them to the tub. The other weasels helped Morton unsnarl the long rope.

"Ready here!" said Morton when the rope was neatly coiled at his feet.

"Me too," said Warton, jumping aboard the tub.

Morton began releasing the rope. The balloon gave a hard jerk, and immediately lifted off the ground.

A powerful wind swept up the face of the cliff and seized the balloon with tremendous force.

Morton suddenly looked horrified. "Warton," he cried, "it's going too fast! I can't hold it back!"

Immediately, the weasels grabbed the rope and, with their greater strength, easily held the balloon back. Then, under Morton's direction, they managed to keep the delicate snakeskins from being ripped open on the jagged edges of the cliff.

Up...up the little craft went. As it rose, everyone kept an eye on the sky, hoping the hawk would not return too soon. In a few moments Warton had a good view of the hawk's nest. He saw that it was mostly a pile of sticks and twigs set in a crotch of a gnarled bush that somehow grew straight out from the side of the cliff. As he drew closer, he could see several bleached bones sticking over the side of the nest. Then he was alongside it. He raised himself and peered over the edge.

There was Freda. Her back was to Warton, and she was scanning the sky intently.

"I've come to get you!" cried Warton.

"That's what *you* think!" cried Freda before she had even turned around. "No oily-feathered hook-beak is going to eat me without getting a few lumps first!" She swung around holding a stout stick over her head.

"Wait!" cried Warton. "It's me!"

Freda was wide-eyed. "What are you doing here? Did that hawk get you too?"

"I'm here to help you get down," said Warton.

"You are?" said Freda. "And how do you expect to do that?"

"In this balloon," said Warton. "Jump in, and they'll pull us down."

Freda looked into the tub, and began to laugh. "Why, you're just as silly as those brothers of mine. I can't fit in that little toad tub. Besides, I'm too heavy—we'd hit the rocks so hard we'd splatter all over the hollow."

Warton suddenly realized Freda was right. In all the excitement, no one had once thought about the size of the washtub. It was barely large enough for two toads. Warton was beginning to feel quite foolish when a great deal of shouting arose from the weasels at the bottom of the cliff.

"Look!" cried Freda, pointing above the distant hills.

Warton saw a speck far off in the sky, and it was coming straight towards them. "It's the hawk!" he cried.

The shouting from below was growing louder and more frantic. The hawk was approaching fast. Warton saw Freda pick up her stick and hold it ready. But he knew she would be no match for the powerful bird. He had to do something immediately . . . but what?

"Freda!" he exclaimed. "Can you pull this tub into the nest?"

Now that the hawk was so much closer, Freda did not seem nearly so brave, and she quickly did as Warton asked.

As soon as the tub was in the nest, Warton set to work untying ropes. When he untied the last one, the snakeskin tubes, as if sensing their freedom,

lifted up. They rose faster and faster till they were high over the nest. Then they disappeared beyond the top of the cliff.

Warton hurriedly untied the long rope from the tub and then retied it to the bush that the nest set upon. "All right," he said to Freda. "Now climb down this rope as fast as you can!"

"Are you sure it's safe?" she said, looking at the ground far below.

"It's safer than staying here," said Warton, watching the hawk coming more swiftly with each beat of his strong wings. There was no time for delay, and he jumped onto the rope. "Look," he shouted to Freda, "it's safe. Now hurry and follow me down!"

The hawk was nearly there, coming in high. He put his wings back and went into a steep dive. Freda waited no longer. She covered her head with the tub and climbed quickly over the edge of the nest just as the hawk reached it. He pulled up sharply and turned around in the sky.

Warton was halfway down with Freda right behind him when he heard the hawk give a terrifying scream. He looked up and saw the hawk go into another dive—this time aiming at the rope.

"Slide!" Warton shouted to Freda. "Slide! It's our only chance!"

He held his breath and loosened his hold on the rope. Faster and faster he went. He looked down and saw the ground coming up at him. He looked up and saw Freda coming down at him. And then he saw the hawk coming straight at him.

The next thing Warton knew, there was a thud and the feeling of thick, soft fur all around as he and Freda, Morton, the other weasels, and the furious hawk all met in one great crash. The air filled with sounds of the weasels, the toads, and the hawk.

Warton, right in the middle of the tumbling mass, saw nothing but flying fur and feathers. Once, for just a moment, he saw the startled face of Morton, as he was turned upside down in mid-air. He heard the clicking of the weasels' sharp teeth and the snapping of the hawk's beak. The screeching and shouting were deafening.

And then ... it stopped.

Warton looked about. With great relief he saw that Morton was safe, though he did look a little dizzy. Fred was sitting on Fritz's stomach. Freda was looking for her bow, which had gotten wrapped around Frank's neck. The rest of the weasels, although a bit battered, seemed all right.

For the next few moments no one said anything. Then, all at once, they each said the same thing. "Where's the hawk?"

As if to answer, from high overhead came a terrible shriek. Everyone looked up. The angry hawk was circling slowly around. He shrieked again and again, but he did not go any lower.

"Look," said Fritz. "He's afraid to attack us again."

Floyd was grinning. "I guess we're too much for him when we all fight together," he said.

There was a sudden silence, and the weasels looked at one another. Then Fulton stood up. "I'm going down to our new home," he said.

"So am I," said Felix.

"Me too," said Farley.

All the other weasels ran after them.

"Hey," yelled Francis, "what about those toads?"

"Let them go," said Fritz. "We don't need them now."

"Well, I'm not sure about that," said Frank. "I've been thinking about having a real toadskin vest."

"Is that so," said Freda. "Well, maybe this will help you think about *not* having one!" She whacked Frank so hard he staggered backwards.

The next thing Warton and Morton knew, the weasels were gone, and they were left standing alone. They looked at each other. Then, without a word, they picked up the tub and started for the stream as fast as they could go.

They had just reached the grassy bank when Morton groaned, "Oh, no! They've changed their minds already."

Warton looked back and saw two weasels racing after them. Quickly, the two toads put the tub into the water. Morton jumped aboard, and Warton prepared to shove off.

the KING of the SKIES

"Wait!" commanded Fred.

"We're going with you," Floyd shouted.

"You are?" said Warton anxiously.

"We're going to walk along the bank of the stream till you reach the safety of the thick woods," said Fred, "where the hawk won't see you."

"Why, that's very nice of you," said Morton, looking surprised.

"It wasn't our idea," said Floyd, as he rubbed a

little bump on the back of his head. "Freda suggested it."

"Oh," chuckled Warton, giving Morton a nudge. Then he pushed the pole against the bank and shoved off. The little tub drifted over the sparkling water and into the deeper part of the stream. There the strong current took hold, and they were swept away.

Around the first bend they came to the hillside where the big wide pine tree grew over what was to be the weasels' new home. Dust was pouring out of the entrance under the stone and swirling up into the air. From inside there came the sound of much commotion.

"Pull that rock out next!" they heard Fulton command.

"Oh, all right," answered Frank. "But remember, next week, when it's my turn, you'd better do what *I* say."

"I'm going to sleep all next week in my own private room," shouted Fritz.

"Good!" yelled Freda. "Then I won't have to cook for you."

Warton and Morton couldn't help but smile.

Then they were swept around another bend, and entered the protective shelter of the thick, over-hanging trees. The moment they did, Fred and Floyd spun around and were gone.

Morton breathed a sigh of relief, and Warton gave one last push with the pole. Then they both settled back and listened to the murmuring of the little stream as it carried them along its winding way to the other side of the deep forest.